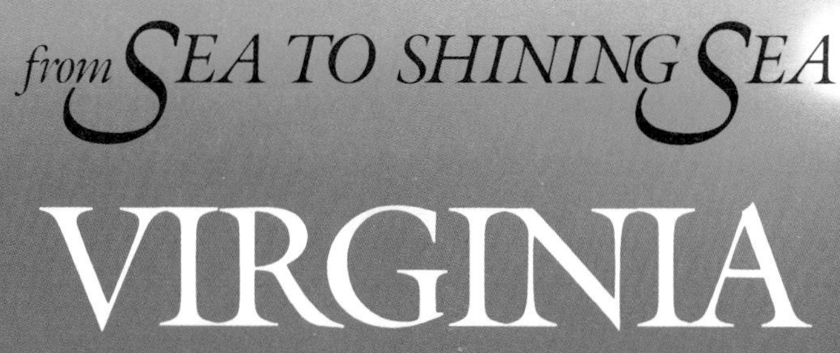

VIRGINIA

By Dennis Brindell Fradin

CONSULTANTS

Nelson D. Lankford, Ph.D., Assistant Director for Publications and Education, Virginia Historical Society

Robert L. Hillerich, Ph.D., Consultant, Pinellas County Schools, Florida; Visiting Professor, University of South Florida

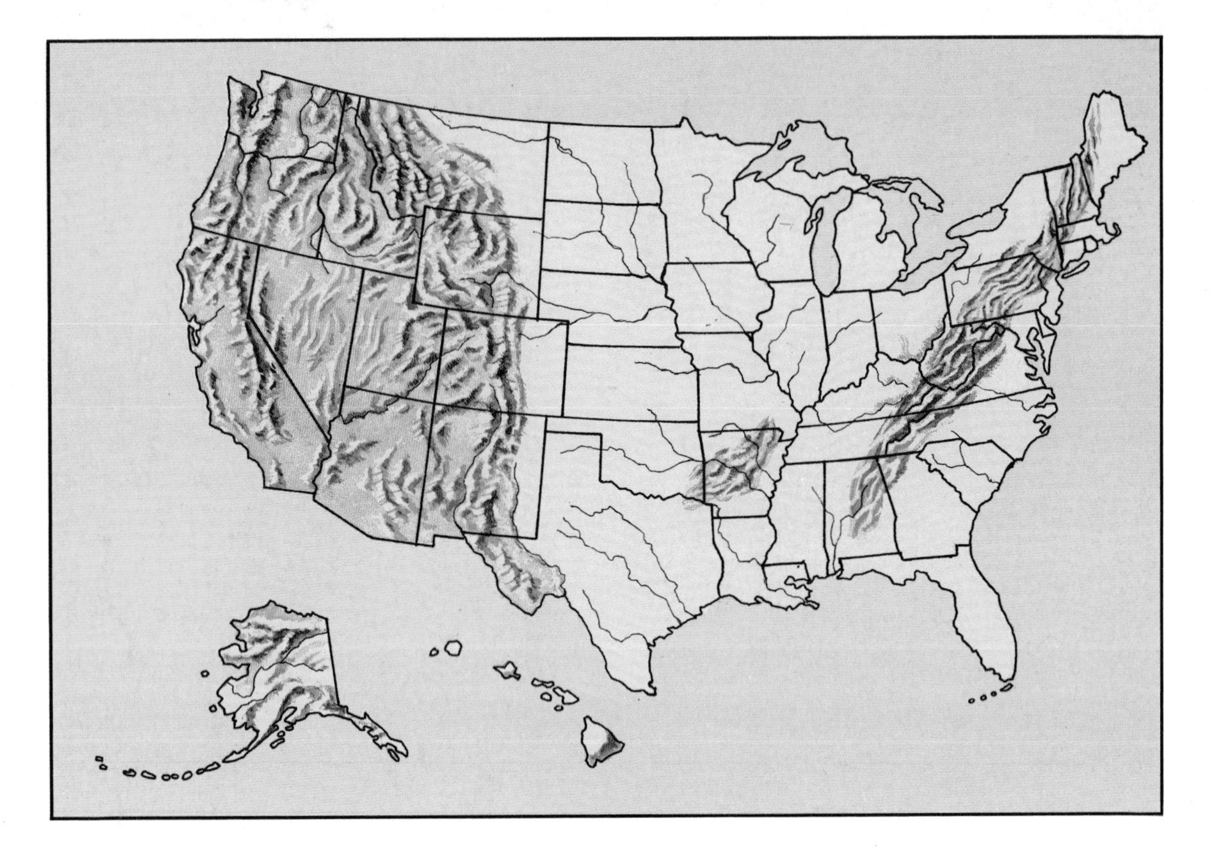

Virginia is one of the fourteen states in the region called the South. The other southern states are Alabama, Arkansas, Delaware, Florida, Georgia, Kentucky, Louisiana, Maryland, Mississippi, North Carolina, South Carolina, Tennessee, and West Virginia.

For my wonderful editor, Joan Downing

Front cover picture: the state capitol, Richmond; page 1, sunrise in the Blue Ridge Mountains, Shenandoah National Park; back cover, a farm near Mt. Olive

Project Editor: Joan Downing
Design Director: Karen Kohn
Research Assistant: Judith Bloom Fradin
Typesetting: Graphic Connections, Inc.
Engraving: Liberty Photoengraving

Printed in the United States of America.
7 8 9 10 R 01 00 99 98 97

Library of Congress Cataloging-in-Publication Data

Fradin, Dennis B.
Virginia / by Dennis Brindell Fradin.
p. cm. — (From sea to shining sea)
Includes index.
Summary: An introduction to the history, geography, important people, and interesting sites of Virginia.
ISBN 0-516-03846-X
1. Virginia—Juvenile literature. [1. Virginia.]
I. Title. II. Series: Fradin, Dennis B.
From sea to shining sea.
F226.3.F67 1992 92-6386
975.5—dc20 CIP
AC

Wild ponies on Assateague Island

Table of Contents

Introducing the Old Dominion

Virginia lies along the East Coast of the United States. It is one of the most historic states. In 1607, Virginia became the first of England's thirteen American colonies. Many years later, the colonists rebelled (fought) against England. Virginian Thomas Jefferson wrote the Declaration of Independence. It explained why the colonists were rebelling. Virginian George Washington led American troops to victory over England. The Revolutionary War's last big battle was fought at Yorktown, Virginia, in 1781.

DUNNINGTON

Eight Virginians have been president of the United States. Virginia has produced more presidents than any other state. For that reason, Virginia is called the "Mother of Presidents." It is also called the "Mother of States." Many states were carved from land that was once Virginia's. But its main nickname is the "Old Dominion." An English king gave Virginia that name long ago.

A picture map of Virginia

Today, Virginia is a manufacturing state. Important products are cigarettes and chemicals. Virginia is a leader at growing tobacco and raising turkeys. It is also a major coal-mining state.

The Old Dominion has other claims to fame. Where was Civil War general Robert E. Lee born? Where did the Civil War end? Where is the government building called the Pentagon found? Which state was the first to elect a black governor? The answer to these questions is: Virginia!

Overleaf: A view from the Blue Ridge Parkway

"A Fruitful and Delightful Land"

"A Fruitful and Delightful Land"

Virginia is shaped like a person's foot. The heel is to the east, touching the Atlantic Ocean. The toes are west, in the Appalachian Mountains. The ankle sticks up to the north.

The Old Dominion is one of the fourteen southern states. Five other southern states border Virginia. Tennessee and North Carolina form Virginia's southern border. Kentucky is to the west. West Virginia curves around the state to the west and northwest. Maryland and Washington, D.C., lie across the Potomac River to the northeast. The Atlantic Ocean and Chesapeake Bay are east of Virginia. The bay separates part of Virginia from the mainland. This small part of Virginia is called the Eastern Shore.

Trilliums in Shenandoah National Park

Mount Rogers is more than a mile tall.

Geography

Virginia has three kinds of land. They are mountains, hills, and coastal plain. The Appalachian Mountains run through western Virginia. Mount Rogers is the state's highest peak. It is in the Blue Ridge range of the Appalachians. Mount Rogers rises 5,729 feet above sea level. Several rivers run through Virginia's Appalachians. Three of them are the Shenandoah, Clinch, and New rivers. The Shenandoah Valley is in the western mountains.

Central Virginia is part of the Piedmont. Virginia's Piedmont is hilly land east of the Appalachians. Several rivers flow southeast across the Piedmont. Some of them are the Potomac, Rappahannock, York, and James rivers.

Piedmont *is a French word. It means "at the foot of the mountains."*

Eastern Virginia is part of the Atlantic Coastal Plain. Virginia's lowest and most level land is there. This area is also called the Tidewater. The ocean's tides wash into Chesapeake Bay. They also flow into the plain's rivers. Across the bay is Virginia's Eastern

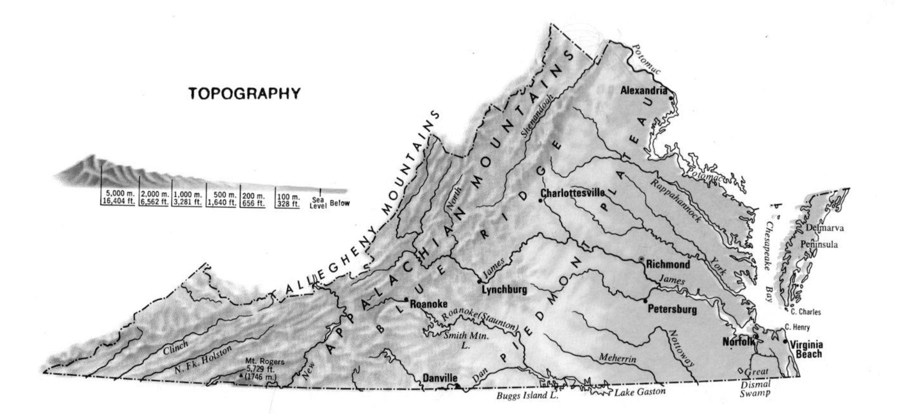

Dark Hollow Falls, in Shenandoah National Park

The Dismal Swamp is at the Virginia-North Carolina border.

Shore. It has many islands. The biggest one is Assateague Island. The Tidewater also has many swamps. The Dismal Swamp is the biggest one.

Woods and Wildlife

The flowering dogwood is Virginia's state tree. Its flowers are the state flower.

Its many forests help make Virginia very lovely. Nearly two-thirds of Virginia is wooded. There are flowering dogwood, hemlock, hickory, and sweet gum trees. Virginia also has ashes, birches, and red cedars.

Deer are common in Virginia's woods. Black bears roam the mountains and swamps. River otters and beavers live along the rivers. Assateague Island is famous for its wild ponies. Foxes, raccoons, weasels, minks, and bobcats also live in Virginia.

Blue jays (below) are common in Virginia.

Many beautiful birds nest in Virginia. There are many cardinals. The cardinal is the state bird. Snow geese winter along the Eastern Shore. Blue jays and robins are common in Virginia. Woodpeckers, ducks, and wild turkeys also live there.

Climate

In general, Virginia has a warm climate. Spring comes early to the Old Dominion. February tem-

Left: Dawn fog at Cumberland Gap
Right: Assateague Island

peratures sometimes reach 50 degrees Fahrenheit. Summers can get hot in Virginia. July temperatures often go above 90 degrees Fahrenheit.

Virginia's autumns are warm and lovely. Many people visit the state each fall. They come just to see the trees turn color. Winters tend to be mild in Virginia. In January, temperatures above freezing (32 degrees Fahrenheit) are common. Some snow does fall, though. From 5 to 10 inches fall along the coast each year. About 2 feet fall in the mountains.

From Ancient Times Until Today

From Ancient Times Until Today

Opposite: Confederate Volunteers of the 1st Virginia Militia (the "Richmond Grays")

Millions of years ago, dinosaurs roamed Virginia. Many of their footprints have been found. In 1989, hundreds of them were found at Culpeper.

American Indians

Prehistoric Indians reached Virginia more than 5,000 years ago. Those ancient Indians hunted deer and bears. Over time, they learned to farm. The Indians planted corn about 2,000 years ago.

Many American Indian groups lived in Virginia before Europeans arrived. The Susquehanna and Powhatan built villages along the coast. The Monacan and Manahoac lived in central Virginia. The Cherokee lived in the western mountains.

Early Virginia Indians often fished for food.

Explorers and First Colonists

Giovanni da Verrazano may have been the first European to reach Virginia. Verrazano was an Italian. But he explored for France. In 1524, he sailed along North America's East Coast.

The name Virginia *honored Queen Elizabeth I. She was called the "Virgin Queen" because she never married.*

Spain was the first nation that tried to settle Virginia. In September 1570, Spanish priests arrived. They built a settlement on the York River. It didn't last long.

The English also explored America. In 1585, they named a large chunk of America *Virginia.*

JAMESTOWN

Left: A statue of Captain John Smith Right: Jamestown, England's first permanent American town, has been partially reconstructed.

In 1606, King James I granted land to the Virginia Company. That company sent 144 Englishmen to Virginia. The Englishmen reached Virginia in May 1607. They built Jamestown. Jamestown became England's first permanent American town.

Jamestown proved to be a poor place to settle. The water tasted bad. The land was swampy. Mosquitoes attacked the settlers and gave them diseases. Many colonists became sick and died.

The colonists weren't farmers. They did not know how to plant crops or hunt game. Soon, they ran short of food. Captain John Smith was a Jamestown leader. He went to many Indian villages. Smith traded mirrors and beads for food. Once, Smith was captured by Powhatan Indians. Their chief, also called Powhatan, ordered that Smith be killed. But Pocahontas, the chief's daughter, begged for Smith's life. The chief spared Smith.

Replicas of the three ships that brought the colonists from England are moored at Jamestown.

More settlers came to Jamestown in 1609. During the winter of 1609-10, hunger set in once again. This was called "the starving time." About 435 of Jamestown's 500 people died.

The Growth of Virginia

In June 1610, more supplies and colonists arrived. The town of Hampton was begun that year. More new towns went up soon afterward.

A colonist named John Rolfe planted a new kind of tobacco in 1612. England paid a lot for Virginia tobacco. Some rich tobacco farmers built plantations. In 1614, John Rolfe married Pocahontas. As a result, the colonists and the Powhatans enjoyed some years of peace.

Tobacco grown in Jamestown was shipped to England.

In 1619, the House of Burgesses was formed. People from Virginia's counties elected representatives. This lawmaking body was America's first elected government.

Also in 1619, the first black people arrived in Virginia. They were indentured servants. Each servant worked for someone for seven years. That work paid for the servant's trip to America. After seven years, the servant was free. Most indentured servants worked on the tobacco plantations.

In the 1620s, hard times once again hit Virginia. The new Powhatan chief led attacks against the colonists. More than 400 colonists were killed. The colonists were too busy fighting Indians to plant crops. The winter of 1622-23 was another "starving time." More than 500 colonists died that winter.

In 1624, the king took Virginia back from the Virginia Company. Virginia became a royal colony. Virginians remained loyal to England's kings for more than 150 years. For its loyalty, King Charles II made Virginia a dominion. He called Virginia his "Old Dominion."

The Old Dominion was one of England's most successful colonies. Large tobacco plantations covered the Tidewater. In the 1640s, the plantation owners needed more workers. They started to buy black slaves in Africa. The slaves were brought to Virginia. There, they worked the land.

A costumed guide tends tobacco at Jamestown.

By the 1650s, colonists started to move west into the Piedmont. Most of them had farms. Some built small plantations. But it was hard to make a living in the Piedmont. The soil wasn't as rich as that in the Tidewater. Besides, Susquehanna Indians now lived in this area. They attacked the colonists. Governor William Berkeley didn't want to fight the Indians. Those western colonists thought the government in Jamestown didn't care about them. They had few representatives in the House of Burgesses.

In 1674, western farmers rebelled against the royal governor. They were led by Nathaniel Bacon. Because of Bacon's Rebellion, Governor Berkeley resigned. The western farmers gained more representatives in the House of Burgesses.

In the 1690s, Williamsburg became Virginia's most important town. In 1693, the College of William and Mary was founded there. In 1699, Williamsburg became the capital. Jamestown had burned nearly to the ground in 1698.

Only Harvard, founded in Massachusetts in 1636, is older than William and Mary.

In the 1700s, Virginia's colonists began to move farther westward. The western mountains had many settlers. Not all of them were English. Many were Irish, Scottish, Welsh, French, and German.

Both England and France wanted to control North America. From 1754 to 1763, they fought the French and Indian War. Large numbers of Indians helped France. Many Virginians helped England win this war.

The Revolutionary War

Patrick Henry (below) was a Revolutionary War patriot.

England needed money. It had debts from the French and Indian War. To raise money, England began taxing the Americans in 1764. The colonists rebelled against these taxes. They felt the taxes were unfair. Then, in 1774, Lord Dunmore closed the House of Burgesses. Dunmore was Virginia's royal governor.

Virginia's Patrick Henry spoke for Americans' rights. He called for a break with England. On March 23, 1775, Henry made a speech in a Richmond church. "Give me liberty or give me death!" he thundered.

The Revolutionary War (1775-1783) began a month later. Americans fought it to break free from

Left: George Washington (standing) at Yorktown
Right: The Yorktown trenches can still be seen.

England. George Washington led the American army.

In October 1781, Washington's forces attacked the English at Yorktown. The English lost 600 men at the Battle of Yorktown. Finally, they gave up on October 19, 1781. America had won its freedom. A peace treaty was signed in 1783.

During the war, American leaders had created the United States of America. Thomas Jefferson of Virginia wrote the Declaration of Independence. It explained why the United States was breaking from England. American leaders approved the declaration on July 4, 1776. Virginia had seven signers: Francis Lightfoot Lee, Benjamin Harrison, Thomas

Ever since the Declaration of Independence was adopted, July 4th has been celebrated as the birthday of the United States.

Jefferson, Carter Braxton, Thomas Nelson, Richard Henry Lee, and George Wythe.

Virginia had become an independent state on June 29, 1776. Its constitution had a bill of rights. George Mason wrote the bill of rights. This listed the rights of all Virginians. Patrick Henry became Virginia's first governor.

THREE FAMOUS "FATHERS"

Below from left to right: James Monroe, Thomas Jefferson, and James Madison, three of the eight Virginians who were president of the United States

In 1787, American leaders wrote the United States Constitution. This is the framework for the country's government. Virginia's James Madison is called the "Father of the Constitution." He guided its cre-

ation. Each state had to approve the Constitution to join the Union. At first, Virginia wouldn't do that. The Constitution didn't have a bill of rights. Finally, Congress agreed to add that later. Virginia finally approved the Constitution. On June 25, 1788, the Old Dominion became the tenth state. Richmond was Virginia's capital, as it still is.

The first president of the United States was elected in 1788. George Washington won easily. He is called the "Father of His Country."

A third famous Virginia "Father" was George Mason. Mason wanted the United States government to protect the people's freedoms. In 1791, Congress adopted the Bill of Rights. It protects freedom of speech, religion, and other rights. Mason became known as the "Father of the Bill of Rights."

The Bill of Rights became the first ten amendments to the Constitution.

Mother of Presidents, Mother of States

John Adams of Massachusetts followed George Washington as president. But Virginians Thomas Jefferson, James Madison, and James Monroe followed Adams. Four of the first five presidents were Virginians!

Later, four more Virginians became president: William Henry Harrison (1841), John Tyler (1841-

1845), Zachary Taylor (1849-1850), and Woodrow Wilson (1913-1921). Only Ohio, with seven, is close to Virginia's record of eight presidents.That's why Virginia is called the Mother of Presidents.

Virginia is also known as the Mother of States. Eight states were carved from Virginia's land: Kentucky, Ohio, Indiana, Illinois, Michigan, Wisconsin, Minnesota, and West Virginia.

Virginia's Slave Trade

By the 1820s, tobacco was losing importance. Planting tobacco year after year had ruined the soil. Plantation owners started to grow cotton and wheat. But those crops didn't earn as much money.

To make more money, some Virginians became slave traders. They bought slaves from tobacco growers who were having hard times. Those slaves were sold to owners in other southern states. Richmond became a big center for selling slaves.

Now and then, slaves rebelled. In 1831, Nat Turner led a revolt in southeastern Virginia. Turner and his followers killed about sixty white people. Nat Turner and about twenty of his followers were hanged. Whites also murdered about a hundred slaves. Those slaves hadn't taken part in the revolt.

The Civil War

By the mid-1800s, slavery had been outlawed in the North. Many northerners wanted the South to end it, too. When Abraham Lincoln became president, some southern states seceded from (left) the Union. They thought that Lincoln would end slavery.

The Civil War cost more American lives than any other war in the nation's history. More than 500,000 Americans died in the war. Virginia was the site of the most bloodshed.

The southern states formed the Confederate States of America (the Confederacy). On April 12, 1861, the Confederates fired on a Union fort. This started the Civil War (1861-1865). The Union (northern states) fought the Confederacy (southern states) in this war. Virginia joined the Confederacy. Richmond became the Confederacy's capital.

Virginian general Robert E. Lee led the Confederate forces. Confederate generals Thomas

Below: Slaves on a southern plantation before the Civil War

"Stonewall" Jackson and Jeb Stuart were also Virginians. About 2,200 of the war's 4,000 battles were fought in Virginia.

The South couldn't win the war. It didn't have enough troops or supplies. On April 9, 1865, General Robert E. Lee surrendered his army. The war ended at Appomattox Court House, Virginia. The Confederate loss had two good results. First, the slaves were freed. Second, the United States was one country again.

Virginian general Robert E. Lee (left) led the Confederates during the Civil War. One southern victory in Virginia was at Chancellorsville (right).

Rebuilding after the War

After the war, Virginia was in ruins. Homes, farms, and railroads had to be rebuilt. Until 1870, United

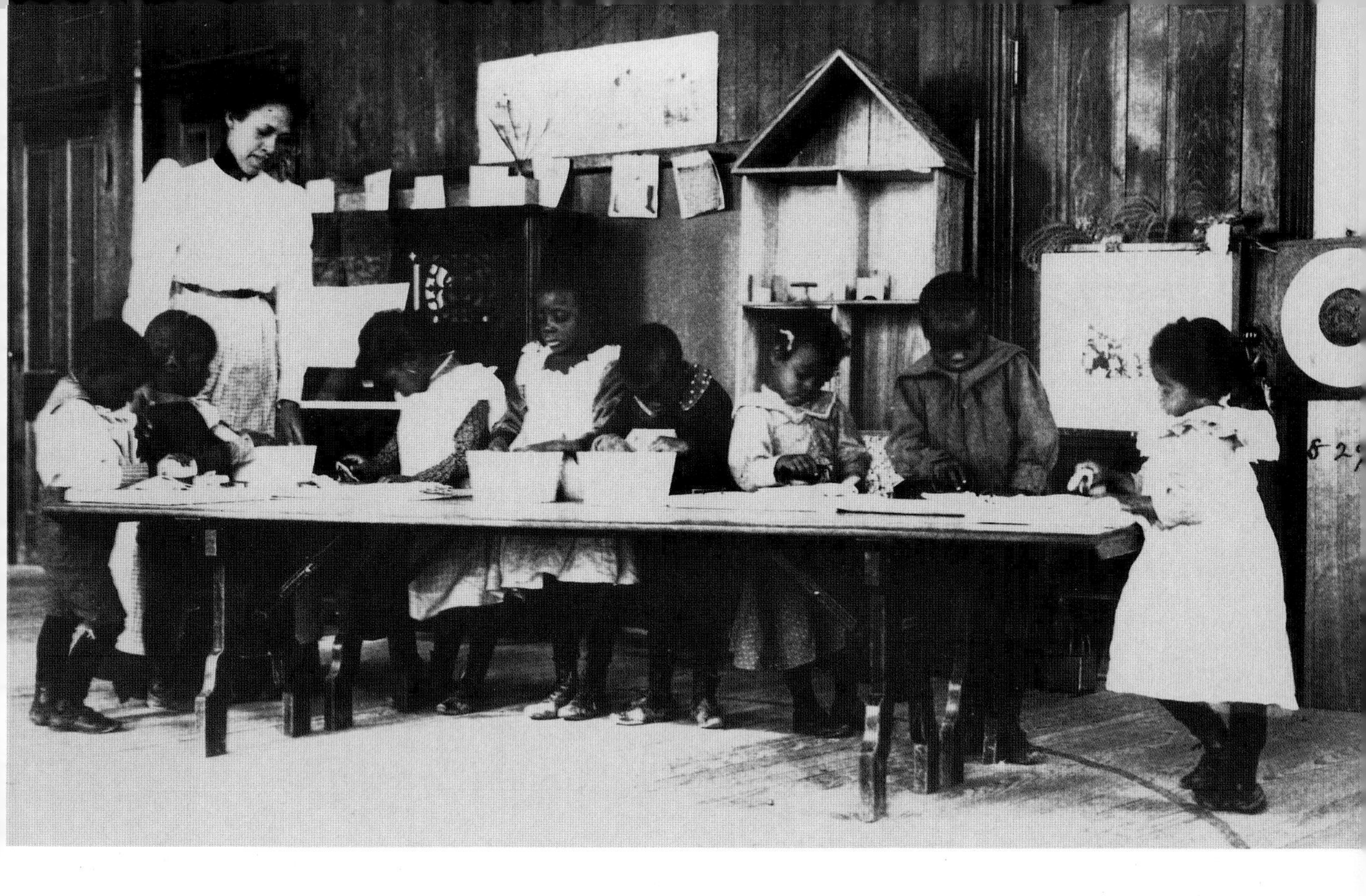

Whittier School (above), was part of Hampton Normal and Agricultural Institute. It was one of the schools founded by the Freedman's Bureau after the Civil War to educate former slaves.

States troops patrolled Virginia. They made sure that Virginia's black people could vote. They also saw that Virginia followed other laws. On January 26, 1870, Virginia rejoined the United States.

New industries helped Virginia recover from the war. They started in the 1880s. Textile (cloth) and furniture plants opened. Cigarette factories were built. Shipbuilding boomed. Rich coal deposits were found in southwest Virginia.

Still, by 1900, poverty was widespread in Virginia. Small farmers had trouble earning a living. Industry still wasn't very well developed.

Virginia placed a new constitution in effect in 1902. It took the vote away from most black Virginians. This kept blacks from electing lawmakers. The state also made laws to separate blacks from whites. Black people had to use separate schools and hotels. They had to sit in separate railroad cars. They were kept from getting good jobs.

Blacks who broke those laws risked being beaten. They could even be lynched (hanged by a mob). Nearly one hundred blacks were lynched in Virginia. This happened between the 1880s and the 1920s. Segregation stayed in force until past 1950.

World Wars and Depression

The United States entered World War I (1914-1918) in 1917. Several military posts opened in Virginia. They included Langley Air Force Base, near Hampton. About 100,000 Virginians served in World War I. Virginians at home helped win the war by making weapons.

Harry Flood Byrd became governor in 1926. He improved Virginia's schools, hospitals, and roads. He also helped make a law that ended lynching in Virginia. Also in 1926, the governor's brother, Richard Evelyn Byrd, flew an airplane over the

Harry and Richard Byrd were both born in Winchester.

North Pole. He and his co-pilot were the first people to do that.

The Great Depression hit America in 1929. It lasted until 1939. Banks failed, factories closed, and farmers lost their farms. Coal mining slowed down. The United States government began new programs. They helped the states survive the Great Depression. One program brought electricity to most Virginia farms.

World War II (1939-1945) helped end the Great Depression. The United States entered the war in 1941. More than 300,000 Virginians served during that war. Seven thousand of them died help-

During the depression, a government relief agency ran this sewing project in Suffolk, Virginia.

ing to win the war. Virginia's factories made weapons. Aircraft carriers and other ships were also made in Virginia.

A New Virginia

Since World War II, Virginia has been changing. By 1950, black southerners were still denied their rights. The United States government began passing laws to end that. In 1954, the Supreme Court ruled that public schools couldn't be segregated. Many Virginians were against that ruling. They set up private schools for white children. Finally, Virginia began to integrate its schools in 1959.

Integrated schools have both black students and white students.

In the 1960s, new laws protected blacks' right to vote. Virginia's blacks elected people who would listen to them. Blacks even began running for public office. In 1977, Henry L. Marsh III became Richmond's first black mayor. In 1989, Virginia's L. Douglas Wilder became the first black governor in the United States.

Manufacturing also helped Virginia. More furniture and clothing factories were built. Plants that made trucks, boats, and ships increased.

Virginia's cities grew. Many farmers moved to the cities. They got jobs in factories. By 1955, more

Virginians lived in cities than in small towns. Today, seven of every ten Virginians live in cities.

Business growth has also brought many new people to the state. They have found jobs there. Between 1980 and 1990, Virginia's population grew by nearly a million people. Virginia is now one of America's fastest-growing areas.

Virginia's growth has caused some problems. Large cities and factories polluted Chesapeake Bay. But the state has started to clean its waters. Efforts to protect plants and animals on the Eastern Shore have begun.

Overleaf: A clam digger at Chincoteague National Wildlife Refuge in Assateague National Seashore

In 1989, Virginia's L. Douglas Wilder (center) became the first black governor in the United States.

Virginians and Their Work

Virginians and Their Work

The 1990 United States Census counted 6,187,358 Virginians. Only eleven of the fifty states have more people.

About three-fourths of Virginia's people are white. Their ancestors came from many countries. Many came from England, Scotland, Ireland, and Germany. Over a million Virginians are black. This is about a fifth of the state's population. Virginia also has about 160,000 Asian Americans and about 160,000 Hispanic Americans.

Costumed guides in Williamsburg help visitors relive history.

Honoring Their Heritage

Virginians are proud of their history. Jamestown and Williamsburg have been restored. There are monuments to Revolutionary War and Civil War events. Virginia has preserved more homes of famous people than any other state.

Virginia has a holiday all its own. It is called Lee-Jackson-King Day. It honors Robert E. Lee, "Stonewall" Jackson, and Martin Luther King, Jr. This holiday is held in January. All three men were born in that month.

Dr. King was born in Georgia, not Virginia. However, he spent his life fighting for the rights of black southerners.

This silversmith is one of the many Virginians who have jobs in colonial Williamsburg.

Their Work

About 3 million Virginians have jobs. That is about half the population. About 750,000 Virginians have service jobs. They include doctors, lawyers, nurses, and hotel workers. About 700,000 Virginians sell goods.

Only nine states have more government workers than Virginia.

About 500,000 Virginians are government workers. Some work for the United States government in Washington, D.C. Others work at navy and air force bases in Virginia.

About 450,000 Virginians work in manufacturing. Chemicals are the state's leading product. Many people also make packaged foods and cigarettes.

Virginians are leading makers of cloth and yarn. Furniture, paper, and plastics are other Virginia products.

Thousands of Virginians fish (left) or farm (right) for a living.

About 50,000 Virginia families farm. Beef cattle are the state's top farm product. Virginia is a leading state for raising turkeys and chickens. The state is still a leader in growing tobacco. Other important crops are peanuts, apples, and cucumbers.

About 200,000 Virginians work at construction. About 15,000 are miners. Coal is the state's number one mining product. Limestone, sandstone, and granite are also mined. A few thousand Virginians fish for a living. They make Virginia a leader at catching oysters and crabs.

Overleaf: The Royal Governors' Palace in Colonial Williamsburg

A Trip Through Virginia

A Trip Through Virginia

Each year, Virginia has about fifty million visitors. This is more tourists than most other states have. But few states offer the beauty and history of Virginia.

The Southeastern Coast

Norfolk (above) is Virginia's second-largest city.

Six of Virginia's eight largest cities lie along its southeastern coast. They are Virginia Beach, Norfolk, Portsmouth, Chesapeake, Newport News, and Hampton.

Virginia Beach is a young city. It began around 1900 as a seaside resort. Since 1963, it has grown rapidly. Today, Virginia Beach is the state's largest city.

As its name shows, the city is famous for its beaches. There are 29 miles of fine sand beaches. They attract visitors from all over the world.

Virginia's first permanent colonists landed at Virginia Beach on April 26, 1607. They founded Jamestown soon afterward. America's first government-built lighthouse is also in Virginia Beach. This is the Old Cape Henry Lighthouse. It was built in 1791-92.

Virginia Beach (above) is a seaside resort city.

The Tidewater Veterans Memorial is a more recent Virginia Beach landmark. Three high school students designed this memorial.

Norfolk was founded in 1682. Today, it is the state's second-largest city. Norfolk is one of America's leading seaports. Millions of tons of cargo pass through Norfolk each year. The Norfolk Naval Base is the world's largest navy base.

Norfolk is home to the Chrysler Museum. Some of its artworks are over five thousand years old. Norfolk Botanical Gardens has beautiful flowers. The International Azalea Festival is held there.

Portsmouth is the state's eighth-biggest city. The Virginia Sports Hall of Fame is there.

Chesapeake is Virginia's fifth-biggest city. The Chesapeake Planetarium is a good place to learn about outer space.

The Dismal Swamp is south of Chesapeake and Portsmouth. Many visitors come to study the plants there. Many others come to hunt and fish.

Newport News is north of Norfolk. It is the state's fourth-largest city. Newport News was settled soon after Jamestown. The world's largest shipbuilding firm is in Newport News. It is called Newport News Shipbuilding. The city is also home to the Mariners Museum. It has exhibits on various kinds of ships.

Below: A carriage driver (left) near the Governor's Palace (right) in colonial Williamsburg.

Hampton is Virginia's sixth-biggest city. It was founded in 1610. Hampton is America's oldest English-built town where people still live. It is home

to Hampton University. This famous mainly black school was founded in 1868.

The Historic Triangle

The Historic Triangle is a short drive northwest of Hampton. Jamestown, Yorktown, and Williamsburg form the triangle. Many famous events in American history occurred in this little area.

The Jamestown settlement of 1607 has been re-created. There are full-size models of the ships that brought the first colonists. A Powhatan village of Pocahontas's time has also been rebuilt.

Above: The Powhatan village at Jamestown

English rule in America began at Jamestown. America won its freedom at nearby Yorktown.

Williamsburg was Virginia's capital from 1699 to 1780. Fifty of the town's buildings have been restored. Thomas Jefferson went to the College of William and Mary in Williamsburg. George Washington made war plans in the Raleigh Tavern. Patrick Henry lived in the Governor's Palace.

The Eastern Shore

The Delmarva Peninsula is east of Chesapeake Bay. This piece of land contains all of Delaware and parts

A soaring egret at Chincoteague National Wildlife Refuge on the Eastern Shore

of Virginia and Maryland. That's where the name *Delmarva* comes from. It uses parts of the words **Del**aware, **Mar**yland, and **V**irgini**a**. Virginians call their part of the peninsula the Eastern Shore.

Cars can reach the Eastern Shore from the Virginia Beach-Norfolk area. They use the 23-mile Chesapeake Bay Bridge-Tunnel. It is the longest bridge-tunnel in the world.

The Eastern Shore has plenty of natural beauty and wildlife. Hundreds of different birds can be seen there. Some of them are snow geese, herons, bald eagles, pelicans, and falcons. Sea turtles swim near the shore. Dolphins and whales swim by.

East of the Delmarva Peninsula is Assateague Island. Many people visit Assateague Island to see its wild ponies. Their ancestors are thought to have survived a Spanish shipwreck. They swam ashore to the island.

RICHMOND

Back on the mainland, Richmond is northwest of Williamsburg. It is Virginia's third-biggest city. Richmond has been Virginia's capital since 1780. Virginia's lawmakers meet in the state capitol there. Thomas Jefferson designed this building. Virginia has the nation's oldest legislature.

The Monument to Famous Virginians (left) and the capitol (right) are highlights of Richmond.

Richmond was also the Confederacy's Civil War capital. The White House of the Confederacy is there. Confederate president Jefferson Davis lived in it. The Museum of the Confederacy is next to this mansion. It has the world's largest collection of Confederate Civil War items. Nearby is the Valentine Museum. It is a museum of the life and history of Richmond. The Virginia Historical Society also has a museum. It covers the state's history since Jamestown.

Edgar Allan Poe was raised in Richmond. He wrote scary short stories and poems. Richmond's Edgar Allan Poe Museum has exhibits about his life.

Northeastern Virginia

Below: Gravestones at Arlington National Cemetery

The two Battles of Manassas were fought in northeastern Virginia. Visitors can tour the battlefield. Northeast of Manassas is Arlington. The Pentagon is in Arlington. It is a five-sided building. The Pentagon is headquarters for the United States Department of Defense.

Thousands of American soldiers are buried in nearby Arlington National Cemetery. The Tomb of the Unknowns is in this cemetery. It holds the remains of four unknown United States soldiers.

This memorial honors all dead American soldiers whose names are unknown.

Alexandria is south of Arlington. It is the state's seventh-biggest city. Robert E. Lee's boyhood home can be visited in Alexandria.

A few miles south of Alexandria is Mount Vernon. This is George Washington's famous home. Nearby is Gunston Hall, home to George Mason. He wrote the Virginia bill of rights.

Left: Manassas National Battlefield
Right: The Tomb of the Unknowns in Arlington National Cemetery
Below: Mount Vernon, George Washington's home

The Piedmont

The hilly Piedmont takes up about the middle third of Virginia. Tobacco, apples, and corn are grown there. Hogs and beef cattle are raised in the Piedmont. Horses for racing and pleasure riding are also raised there.

Charlottesville is in the Piedmont. Thomas Jefferson founded the University of Virginia there in 1819. He also designed the school's main buildings. Monticello, Jefferson's home, is outside Charlottesville. Jefferson also designed his home. Two of Jefferson's friends lived near Monticello. They also became presidents of the United States. James Madison's home is called Montpelier. James Monroe lived at a home called Ash Lawn-Highland.

Monticello, Thomas Jefferson's home

Appomattox Court House National Historical Park is southwest of Charlottesville. The Civil War ended there. Patrick Henry's home is south of Appomattox. It is called Red Hill.

The Mountainous West

Western Virginia also has a Shenandoah river, valley, county, and town. The name Shenandoah *comes from* Shanando, *an Indian word meaning "daughter of the stars."*

The Appalachian Mountains run through western Virginia. There are many little towns and farms in the mountains and valleys. Beef cattle and sheep are raised in these regions. Rockingham County is famous for raising turkeys and broiler chickens.

Shenandoah National Park is in the Blue Ridge Mountains of western Virginia. This famous park is a great place for hiking and exploring. Skyline Caverns are north of the park. There, many stone formations look like flowers. Luray Caverns are just west of the park. The stone formations there come in many colors and shapes. South of Luray Caverns is Staunton. President Woodrow Wilson was born there. Visitors can see the twenty-eighth president's home.

Luray Caverns (below) contain many beautiful stone formations.

Lexington is a short drive southwest of Wilson's birthplace. Two famous colleges are in Lexington. One is the Virginia Military Institute (VMI). "Stonewall" Jackson taught science at VMI before the Civil War. The other college is Washington and Lee University. Robert E. Lee served as this school's president after the Civil War.

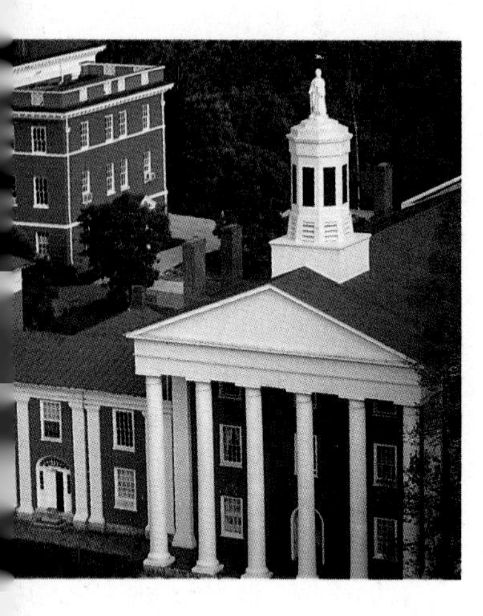

Washington and Lee University (above) was named for George Washington and Robert E. Lee.

South of Lexington is Natural Bridge. This town is named after a stone bridge. Water ate away soft rock over time. A natural bridge was left behind. Thomas Jefferson liked it so much that he bought it. He built a log cabin there.

Roanoke is southwest of Natural Bridge. In the 1880s, Roanoke became an important railroad center. The Virginia Museum of Transportation is there. It has a railroad exhibit. Railroad cars are made in the city today. Clothing, steel, and furniture are also made there.

Long ago, mountain families were cut off from the world. They had to make their own household goods. These mountain crafts are still alive today. Some families make their own clothes, quilts, baskets, and pottery. Abingdon is in southwestern Virginia. The town hosts a yearly craft show. It is called the Virginia Highlands Festival.

East of Abingdon is Galax. It hosts the Old Fiddler's Convention each August. Visitors enjoy folk songs and dancing. Natural Tunnel is west of Abingdon, near Gate City. Creek waters slowly carved this tunnel through a mountain.

Cumberland Gap National Historical Park is in Virginia's far southwest corner. It is a good place to end a Virginia trip. The Cumberland Gap is a pass in the Appalachian Mountains. Virginia, Tennessee, and Kentucky meet at this pass. The ancestors of millions of Americans passed through Cumberland Gap. It was an easy way for Virginians to get through the mountains. Those people helped settle the lands west of Virginia.

Left: Natural Bridge, south of Lexington
Right: Musicians at the Johnson farm, near the Peaks of Otter

A Gallery of Famous Virginians

A Gallery of Famous Virginians

Few states have produced as many famous people as Virginia. Many of America's leaders have been Virginians. Explorers and inventors have come from the state. Virginia has also produced writers, entertainers, and athletes.

Powhatan (about 1547-1618) was a powerful Indian chief of eastern Virginia. At first, he wanted to drive the settlers away. Powhatan became friendly after his daughter Pocahontas married settler John Rolfe.

George Washington (1732-1799) was born in Virginia. He became a surveyor. Later, he became a soldier. His first war was the French and Indian War. Washington later became the "Father of His Country."

Another Virginia soldier was **George Rogers Clark** (1752-1818). He was born near Charlottesville. During the Revolutionary War, Clark led Virginia troops. They won battles against the English in present-day Illinois and Indiana.

Opposite: A painting by J. L. G. Ferris of artist Gilbert Stuart painting his "Athenaeum" portrait of George Washington

Henry Lee (1756-1818) was born in Prince William County. During the Revolutionary War, Lee led a troop of horse soldiers. He struck so

Robert E. Lee (with binoculars) was commander of the Confederate army.

No other chief justice served as long as John Marshall (below).

quickly that he was called "Lighthorse Harry." Later, Lee was Virginia's governor (1792-1795).

Robert E. Lee (1807-1870) was "Lighthorse Harry's" son. Lee became a soldier. He commanded the Confederate army. Lee led it bravely and well.

John Marshall (1755-1835) was born in Fauquier County. He fought in the Revolutionary War. Marshall was chief justice of the U.S. Supreme Court (1801-1835).

The exploring team of Lewis and Clark also came from Virginia. **Meriwether Lewis** (1774-1809) and **William Clark** (1770-1838) explored the northwestern part of the United States (1804-1806). They helped open that land to settlement.

Inventors and scientists also were born in Virginia. **Cyrus McCormick** (1809-1884) was born near Lexington. He invented the McCormick reaper. Farmers used this machine to harvest wheat. **Walter Reed** (1851-1902) was born near Yorktown. He was a famous doctor. Reed learned how typhoid fever and yellow fever are spread.

Virginia has produced many black leaders. **Booker T. Washington** (1856-1915) was born on a plantation near Roanoke. He was a slave until the age of nine. In 1881, he founded what is now Tuskegee University, in Alabama. It is one of the nation's most famous mainly black universities.

Carter Woodson (1875-1950) was born in New Canton. He became a great black leader. Dr. Woodson helped found Black History Month.

Maggie Walker (1867-1934) was born in Richmond. Her mother had been a slave. Walker founded a bank in Richmond. She became America's first woman bank president.

Many Virginians have become famous writers. Richmond-born **Ellen Glasgow** (1874-1945) became a famous author. She wrote novels about southern life. Novelist **William Styron** was born in Newport News in 1924. He wrote *The Confessions of Nat Turner*. It is about the famous slave revolt in 1831. Children's author **William Howard Armstrong** was born near Lexington in 1914. He

Booker T. Washington

Ellen Glasgow (below) and William Styron both won Pulitzer Prizes for fiction.

won the 1970 Newbery Medal for his famous novel *Sounder.*

The great dancer **Bill "Bojangles" Robinson** (1878-1949) was born in Richmond. He danced in films with child star Shirley Temple. Jazz singer **Ella Fitzgerald** was born in Newport News in 1918.

Movie star **Shirley MacLaine** was born in Richmond in 1934. Her brother **Warren Beatty** was born there in 1938. In 1983, MacLaine won an Academy Award for best actress. Beatty won an Academy Award for best director in 1981.

Great athletes have also come from Virginia. Golfing great **Sam Snead** was born near Hot Springs in 1912. "Slammin' Sammy" won more than 150 tournaments. That is more than any other

Shirley MacLaine (left) and Ella Fitzgerald (right) were born in Virginia

Left: Golfing great Sam Snead is on the right in this photo. Right: Tennis star Arthur Ashe

American golfer. **Fran Tarkenton** was born in Richmond in 1940. He was a pro football star. Tarkenton threw 342 touchdown passes in his career. That is more than any other quarterback. Tennis star **Arthur Ashe** (1943-1993) was born in Richmond. In 1968, he won the U.S. men's singles tennis title. Ashe was the first black man to do that.

Home to Patrick Henry, Booker T. Washington, Pocahontas, Thomas Jefferson, and Maggie Walker . . .

The place where the thirteen colonies began, where the Revolutionary War was won, and where the Civil War ended . . .

The state that has the Natural Bridge, the Natural Tunnel, and the Blue Ridge Mountains . . .

Mother of Presidents, Mother of States, and home to the Father of His Country . . .

This is Virginia—the Old Dominion.

Did You Know?

Bill "Bojangles" Robinson had another talent besides dancing. He could run backward very fast. He once set a world record by running backward 75 yards in 8.2 seconds.

Mary Ball Washington was the mother of the "Father of His Country." When the Revolutionary War began, she reportedly said: "Oh these men. Must they always be fighting and killing each other?"

In 1856, Henry Brown, a Virginia slave, made an unusual escape. He was placed in a box with food and water and mailed north to Philadelphia. When the box arrived, Brown stepped out to freedom. He became known as "Box" Brown.

As a young man, Patrick Henry hardly seemed headed for greatness. He had failed at one job after another. He spent much of his time playing the fiddle in his father-in-law's tavern. Patrick found the road to success when he took up law at age twenty-three.

Virginia's state song, "Carry Me Back to Old Virginia," was written by James A. Bland, a black man who was homesick for Virginia.

Marguerite Henry wrote a famous children's novel about the ponies along the Eastern Shore. It is called *Misty of Chincoteague*.

As a boy, George Washington supposedly chopped down a cherry tree. He admitted this to his father with the words: "I cannot tell a lie." The truth is, an author made up this story. Yet, to this day, many people bake cherry pies on Washington's birthday (February 22).

The New River of western Virginia is actually one of North America's oldest rivers.

Virginia has towns called Triangle, Horse Pasture, and Pocahontas.

Virginian Edmund Ruffin fired the first shot of the Civil War on April 12, 1861, at Charleston, South Carolina, in an attack on a Union fort. Ruffin was sixty-seven years old at the time.

William Henry Harrison served the shortest term of any United States president. Harrison caught a cold the day he became president. He died of pneumonia thirty days later.

The first English child born in America entered the world in 1587 in present-day North Carolina. She was named Virginia Dare because her birthplace was then part of Virginia. But Virginia didn't become a popular girls' name in the United States until about 1900.

Virginia Information

State flag

Area: 40,767 square miles (thirty-sixth biggest state of the fifty states)

Greatest Distance North to South: 200 miles

Greatest Distance East to West: 470 miles

Borders: Kentucky to the west; West Virginia to the west and the northwest; Maryland and Washington, D.C., to the northeast; Chesapeake Bay and the Atlantic Ocean to the east; and North Carolina and Tennessee to the south

Flowering dogwood

Highest Point: Mount Rogers in the Blue Ridge Mountains, 5,729 feet above sea level

Lowest Point: Sea level, along the Atlantic Ocean

Hottest Recorded Temperature: 110° F. (at Columbia, on July 5, 1900, and also near Glasgow, on July 15, 1954)

Coldest Recorded Temperature: -30° F. (near Blacksburg, on January 22, 1985)

Statehood: The tenth state, on June 25, 1788

Origin of Name: The name Virginia honors England's Queen Elizabeth I, who was known as the "Virgin Queen"

Capital: Richmond

Counties: 95

Cardinal

United States Senators: 2

United States Representatives: 11 (as of 1992)

State Senators: 40

State Delegates: 100

State Song: "Carry Me Back to Old Virginia," by James A. Bland

State Motto: *Sic Semper Tyrannis* (Latin, meaning "Thus always to tyrants")

Nicknames: "Old Dominion," "Mother of Presidents," "Mother of States"

American foxhounds

State Seal: Adopted in 1931
State Flag: Adopted in 1931
State Flower: Flowering dogwood
State Bird: Cardinal
State Tree: Flowering dogwood
State Dog: American foxhound
State Shell: Oyster shell

Some Rivers: Potomac, York, James, Rappahannock, Shenandoah, Roanoke, Clinch, New

Wildlife: Deer, black bears, foxes, raccoons, rabbits, river otters, beavers, skunks, weasels, minks, bobcats, wild ponies, cardinals, blue jays, robins, hummingbirds, woodpeckers, snow geese, ducks, wild turkeys, herons, bald eagles, pelicans, peregrine falcons, many other kinds of birds, oysters, crabs, clams, trout, bass, catfish, many other kinds of fish, sea turtles

Manufacturing Products: Chemicals, cloth and yarn, packaged foods, cigarettes, furniture, paper, plastics, ships, electrical equipment

Farm Products: Beef cattle, turkeys, broiler chickens, sheep, horses, hogs, eggs, milk, tobacco, peanuts, apples, cucumbers, peaches, corn, soybeans, hay, wheat, barley, tomatoes

Mining Products: Coal, limestone, granite, sand and gravel

Population: 6,187,358, twelfth among the fifty states (1990 U.S. Census Bureau figures)

Major Cities (1990 Census):

Virginia Beach	393,069	Hampton	133,793
Norfolk	261,229	Alexandria	111,183
Richmond	203,056	Portsmouth	103,907
Newport News	170,045	Roanoke	96,397
Chesapeake	151,976	Lynchburg	66,049

Turkeys

Pelican

Virginia History

The College of William and Mary was founded in 1693

3000 B.C.—Prehistoric Indians reach Virginia

A.D. 1524—Giovanni da Verrazano sails along the Virginia coast

1570—Spanish priests build a settlement on the York River

1607—England's first permanent American settlement is founded at Jamestown

1610—Hampton is begun

1619—The House of Burgesses, America's first elected government, is formed in Jamestown

1650—Virginia's colonial population is about 20,000

1693—The College of William and Mary is founded

1699—Williamsburg replaces Jamestown as the capital

1736—Virginia's first newspaper, the *Virginia Gazette*, is founded

1754-63—Virginia soldiers, including George Washington, help England win the French and Indian War

1764—England begins taxing Americans to help pay its debts

1775—Patrick Henry makes his "Liberty or Death" speech in Richmond; the Revolutionary War begins

1776—Thomas Jefferson writes the Declaration of Independence, which is approved on July 4

1780—Richmond becomes Virginia's capital

1781—The English give up at Yorktown, Virginia

1783—The peace treaty is signed, officially ending the war

1787—James Madison guides the creation of the U.S. Constitution

1788—Virginia becomes the tenth state on June 25

1789—George Washington becomes the first U.S. president

1801—Thomas Jefferson becomes the third U.S. president

1809—James Madison becomes the fourth U.S. president

1817—James Monroe becomes the fifth U.S. president

1819—Thomas Jefferson founds the University of Virginia, at Charlottesville

1831—Nat Turner leads a slave revolt

1841—William Henry Harrison becomes the ninth U.S. president but dies a month later; another Virginian, John Tyler, then becomes the tenth U.S. president

1849—Zachary Taylor becomes the twelfth U.S. president

1850—The population of Virginia is almost 1,120,000

1861—The Civil War begins; Virginia secedes from the Union

1865—The Civil War ends with Confederate general Robert E. Lee surrendering at Appomattox Court House

1870—Virginia is readmitted into the United States

1913—Woodrow Wilson becomes the twenty-eighth U.S. president

1917-18—After the United States enters World War I, about 100,000 Virginians serve

1929-39—During the Great Depression, factories close, farms go out of business, and coal mining slumps in Virginia

1941-45—After the United States enters World War II, more than 300,000 Virginians serve

1959—Virginia begins to integrate its schools

1964—The Chesapeake Bay Bridge-Tunnel is completed

1976—Lawrence A. Davies and Noel C. Taylor are elected the first black mayors of Virginia cities

1977—Henry L. Marsh III is elected Richmond's first black mayor

1988—Virginia celebrates its two hundredth birthday as a state

1990—L. Douglas Wilder becomes the nation's first black governor; Virginia's population reaches 6,187,358

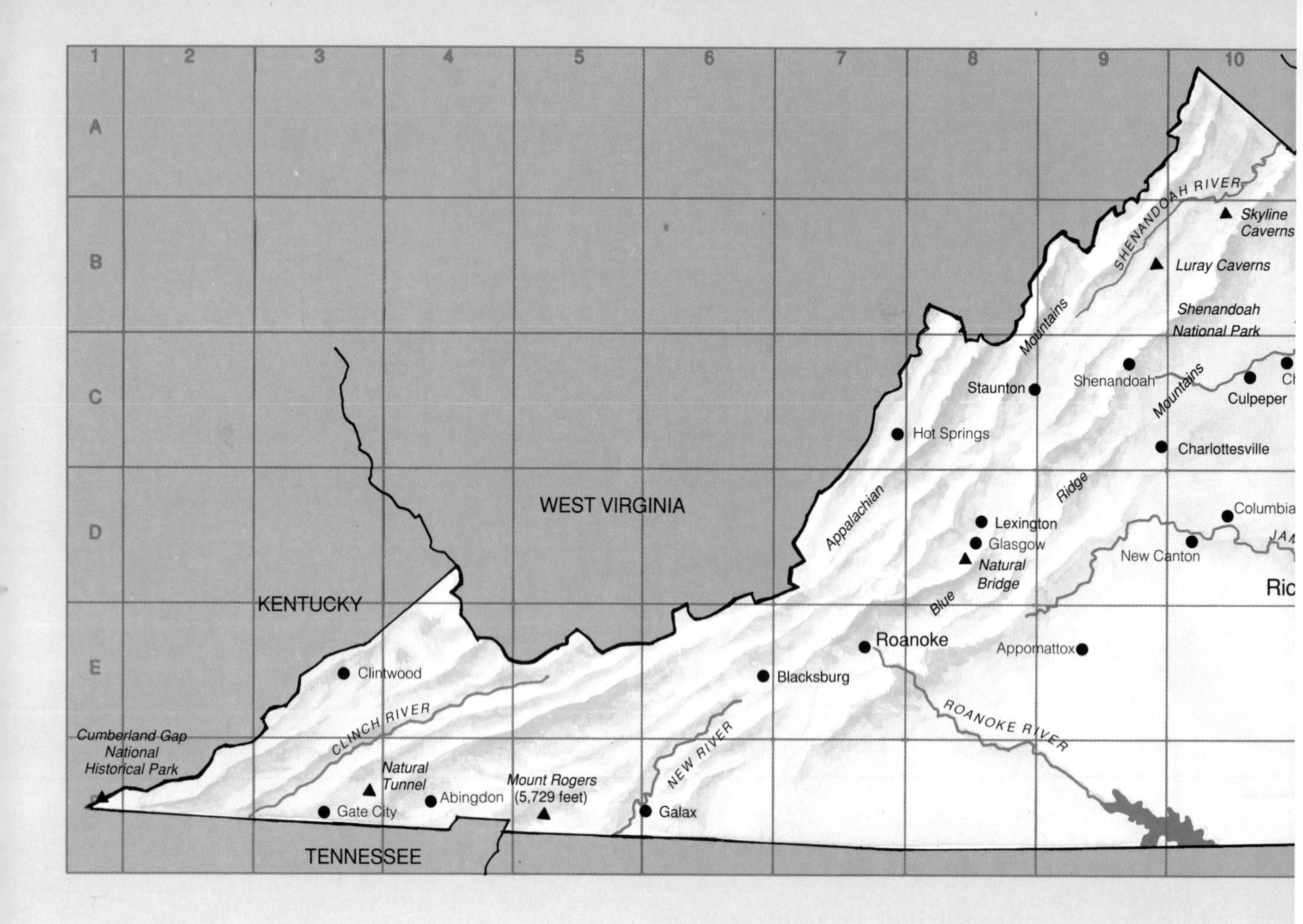

MAP KEY

Abingdon F4
Alexandria B11
Appalachian Mountains B,C,D7,8,9
Appomattox E9
Arlington B11
Assateague Island C,D14
Atlantic Ocean D,E14
Blacksburg E6
Blue Ridge Mountains C,D8,9,10
Chancellor C10
Charlottesville C9
Chesapeake F13
Chesapeake Bay C,D13
Chesapeake Bay Bridge-Tunnel E14
Clinch River E,F3,4
Clintwood E3
Columbia D10
Culpeper C10
Cumberland Gap National Historical Park F1
Delmarva Peninsula D13,14
Dismal Swamp F13
Fredericksburg C11
Galax F5
Glasgow D8
Gate City F3
Hampton E13
Hot Springs C7
James River D10,11
Jamestown E12
Lexington D8
Luray Caverns B9
Manassas B11
Mount Rogers F5
Mount Vernon B11
Natural Bridge D8
Natural Tunnel F3
New Canton D10
New River E,F6
Newport News E13
Norfolk E13
Petersburg E11

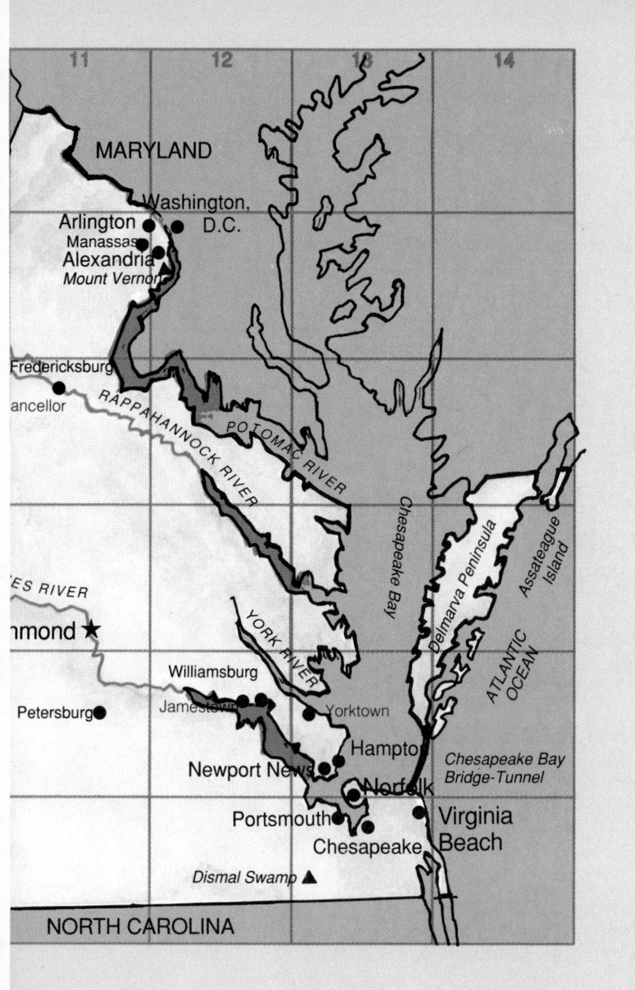

Portsmouth	F13
Potomac River	C12,13
Rappahannock River	C11,12
Richmond	D11
Roanoke	E7
Roanoke River	E,F8,9
Shenandoah	C9
Shenandoah National Park	B10
Shenandoah River	A,B9,10
Skyline Caverns	B10
Staunton	C8
Virginia Beach	F13
Williamsburg	E12
York River	D,E12,13
Yorktown	E13

Glossary

ancestor: A person from whom one is descended, such as a grandfather or a great-grandmother

ancient: Relating to a time early in history

capital: The city that is the seat of government

capitol: The building in which the government meets

cavern: Cave

colonist: A person who settles in a region outside the parent country

colony: A settlement that is outside a parent country and that is ruled by the parent country

constitution: A framework of government

debt: Money that is borrowed from another person or country and that must be paid back

dominion: A colony or other region ruled by a king or queen

explorer: A person who visits and studies unknown lands

export: To ship goods out of a state or country

independence: Freedom from the control of others

industry: A kind of business in which many workers make products

integration: The process of bringing people of various races together

legislature: A lawmaking body or bodies

manufacturing: The making of products

peninsula: Land that is almost surrounded by water

plantation: A huge southern farm

population: The number of people in a place

representative: A person who is elected to serve others in a lawmaking body

segregation: The process of keeping people apart because of their race or some other reason

slavery: A practice in which some people are owned by other people

surveyor: Someone who measures land boundaries

PICTURE ACKNOWLEDGMENTS

Front cover, © **Gene Ahrens;** 1, © **Tom Till/Photographer;** 2, **Tom Dunnington;** 3, © **Mary Ann Brockman;** 4-5, **Tom Dunnington;** 6-7, © **Tom Dietrich;** 8, © Willard Clay/**Tony Stone Worldwide/Chicago, Ltd.;** 9 (left), **courtesy of Hammond, Incorporated, Maplewood, New Jersey;** 9 (right), © **Tom Dietrich;** 10, © John Gerlach/**Tom Stack & Associates;** 11 (left), © **Gene Ahrens;** 11 (right), © Gene Ahrens/**SuperStock;** 12, **Valentine Museum, Richmond, Virginia;** 13, **North Wind Picture Archives, hand colored;** 14 (left), © **James P. Rowan;** 14 (right), © Richard L. Capps/**R/C Photo Agency;** 15, © **SuperStock;** 16, **Historical Pictures/Stock Montage;** 17, © **Mary Ann Brockman;** 18, **courtesy Colonial Williamsburg Foundation;** 19 (left), **North Wind Picture Archives, hand colored;** 19 (right), © **SuperStock;** 20 (left and middle), **Historical Pictures/Stock Montage;** 20 (right), **North Wind Picture Archives, hand colored;** 23, **Illinois State Historical Library;** 24 (left), **Virginia State Library and Archives;** 24 (right), **Historical Pictures/Stock Montage;** 25, **Hampton University Archives;** 27, **Richmond Newspapers Inc., from Virginia State Library and Archives;** 29, **AP/Wide World Photos;** 30, © **Mary Ann Brockman;** 31, © **Cameramann International, Ltd.;** 32, © **Cameramann International, Ltd.;** 33 (left), © **SuperStock;** 33 (right), © **Tom Dietrich;** 34-35, © **Clemenz Photography;** 36, © Doris DeWitt/**Tony Stone Worldwide/Chicago, Ltd.;** 37, © J. Blank/**H. Armstrong Roberts;** 38 (left), © **Cameramann International, Ltd.;** 38 (right), © F. Sieb/**H. Armstrong Roberts;** 39, © Charlie Borland/**Charlie Borland Stock;** 40, © **Mary Ann Brockman;** 41 (left), © David M. Doody/**Tom Stack & Associates;** 41 (right), © Henley & Savage/**Tony Stone Worldwide/Chicago, Ltd.;** 42, © **Tom Dietrich;** 43 (top left), © **Charlie Borland-WildVision;** 43 (top right), © **Mae Scanlan;** 43 (bottom), © B. Kulik/**Photri;** 44, © **Photri;** 45, **Virginia Division of Tourism;** 46, © **SuperStock;** 47 (left), © James Blank/**Root Resources;** 47 (right), © **Tom Dietrich;** 48, **J.L.G. Ferris, Archives of 76, Bay Village, Ohio;** 49, **North Wind Picture Archives;** 50 (top), **Tulane University Library;** 50 (bottom), **Historical Pictures/Stock Montage;** 51 (both pictures), **Historical Pictures/Stock Montage;** 52 (both pictures), **AP/Wide World Photos;** 53 (both pictures), **AP/Wide World Photos;** 54, **AP/Wide World Photos;** 55 (left), **North Wind Picture Archives;** 55 (right), **Historical Pictures/Stock Montage;** 56 (top), **courtesy Flag Research Center, Winchester, Massachusetts 01890;** 56 (middle), © **Mary Ann Brockman;** 56 (bottom), © Anthony Mercieca Photo/**Root Resources;** 57 (top), © Lani N. Howe/**Photri;** 57 (middle), © **SuperStock;** 57 (bottom), © Ben Goldstein/**Root Resources;** 58, © Doris DeWitt/**Tony Stone Worldwide/Chicago, Ltd.;** 60, **Tom Dunnington;** back cover, © **Tom Dietrich**

INDEX

Page numbers in boldface type indicate illustrations.

About the Author

Dennis Brindell Fradin is the author of 150 published children's books. His works for Childrens Press include the Young People's Stories of Our States series, the Disaster! series, and the Thirteen Colonies series. Dennis is married to Judith Bloom Fradin, who taught high-school and college English for many years. She is now Dennis's chief researcher. The Fradins are the parents of two sons, Anthony and Michael, and a daughter, Diana. Dennis graduated from Northwestern University in 1967 with a B.A. in creative writing, and has lived in Evanston, Illinois, since that year.